Friends Are Full of Surprises

Metro Early Reading Program

Level B, Stories 6–10

Credits
Illustration: Front cover, Lane Gregory
Photography: Front and back covers, Mark Segal/Tony Stone Images

ISBN 1-58120-647-X

1 2 3 4 5 6 7 8 9 02 01 00 99

Table of Contents

You Can Do a Lot with a Lot

3

You do not have to feed Mop.
Your dad will feed her for you.

5

6

They are just some old tin cans.
I have to put them in the bin.
Come and work with me, Lin.
This is a chore you will like.

7

9

It is a weed.
We need to dig
them all up.
Would you like to
work with us,
Tasha?

We have to dig up
all the weeds.
Then we can put
seeds in the soil.
After that, we can
water them.

13

16

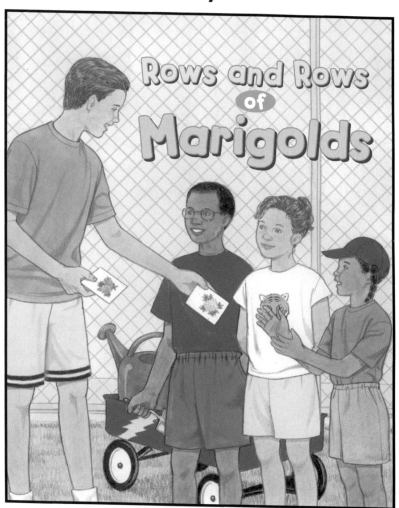

Rows and Rows of Marigolds

18

19

Marigolds grow from seeds.
I will show you how to sow seeds.
One, we dig a row.
Two, we put seeds in the row we made.
Three, we put soil on the seeds.

22

23

24

25

28

The seeds need sun.
The seeds need a lot
more water.
There are no marigolds
yet.
But little by little, the
marigolds will grow.

Story 8

Boo, you have not been here before. Come with me and see the marigolds. They were just seeds before.

All of us can weed.
Boo can nap by the marigolds.
He will be fine there.

36

39

That red van is mine.
I know a good vet.
It will not take long
to get there.

44

Boo did not like the ride here.
I hope he likes the vet better
than the van.
He has not been to this vet.

45

Boo is much better than before.
The vet said he will be fine.
But he can not go up any more vines.

47

48

Make My Day

52

53

We will put the fake bug on his face.
Then we will buzz like a bug.
Carlos will wake up and see the fake bug.
Then he will hop out of bed!

55

He will hop out of bed.
But he will hop out mad.
Do not play that joke
on Carlos.

57

58

61

63

The Surprise Birthday

67

Get the cake box and the pan, Jed. We will need to put in water. This mug would be good for water.

70

You two do not know how to bake. Your mom will come in a little bit, Ben. She will show you what to do.

71

All you do is whine, Carlos.
Whine, whine, whine.
We will just put in the water, Carlos.
That is all we will do.

72

73

74

75

How come there is
so much in the pan?
What did you put
in the cake?
I do not know about
this cake.
But I will bake it
for you.

76

77

81

83

85

87

89

90

Story 6: You Can Do a Lot with a Lot

New

initial digraph:
ch

phonograms:
-eed, -ore

decodable words:
bin, chore, dig, feed, more, need, seed, weed

sight word:
them

story words:
soil, water

Skills and Vocabulary

Story 7: Rows and Rows of Marigolds

New

initial digraph:
sh-

phonograms:
-ade, -ow

decodable words:
made, row, show, sow, yet

sight word:
many

story words:
grow, marigold

Skills and Vocabulary

Story 8: Get Down from That Vine

First Review

initial consonant:

v

New

phonograms:

-ine, -ope

decodable words:

fine, hope, mine, van, vet, vine

sight words:

been, than, were

story words:

better, hurt

Skills and Vocabulary

Story 9: Make My Day

New

initial digraph:
wh-

phonograms:
-ake, -oke

decodable words:
face, fake, joke, wake, wham

story word:
movie

Story 10: The Surprise Birthday

Review Story

No new phonics elements or sight words.